Maryja

Daniela Králová

Published by Daniela Králová, 2024.

MARYJA

First edition. November 15, 2024.

Copyright © 2024 Daniela Králová.

ISBN: 979-8230265474

Written by Daniela Králová.

Table of Contents

Just as a snake sheds its skin, we must shed our past over
and over again.

-The Buddha

A Sinuous Discovery

The wicker chair creaked on the porch as Idris Schopenhauer pulled his stomach in, forcing his shoulders back. He brought the pipe to his lips, inhaling, exhaling coils of smoke. Birds settled into their nests for the evening, their trilling interrupted by his cough. It was late spring, petals beautifying the concrete.

Maryja hung her head over the edge of the sink, shutting the drafty window. The kitchen made her thoughts stuffy, but her legs knew to carry her as her hands prepared dinner. She twisted her face towards her underarms. Like a horse or cur; meat, sinew, labor. Sweat dripped into her eyes. She squeezed them shut, everything bright again.

The red-haired woman leaped up, sun-bleached book in her hands. A girl with a long mousy braid ran around her in circles, screaming with delight as the woman reached out to snatch her and missed. Rows of herbs tempered the heavy sweet of the lavender that barred their home from outside world. Insects swarmed the pond near the bower of the willow tree, its drooped white tendrils swaying. They sheltered Maryja as snakes rounded in the grass.

"'Do you not know that I am a woman? When I think, I must speak.'" The red-haired woman laughed.

The two continued their happy play; Maryja watched in quiet contentment. When the act ended they retreated inside to the warm fire of the cottage, smoking thinly out over the garden.

"Marija, come inside! Marija..."

"...Maryja!"

Opening her eyes, Maryja reemerged before the rising heat. With greasy hands she lifted the hem of her blue dress and scuffled onto the porch. She curtseyed, her eyes on Idris's breast pocket, from which his Ministry pin proudly shone— fiery gem, sun of his universe.

"Minister."

The cur smell returned, impatient bubbles of the boiling stew making the stovetop hiss. Maryja kept her place, not yet dismissed.

A tall, gaunt Godfellow made his way up the steps. His sharp cheekbones and yellowish eyes contrasted sharply to Idris's tan, paunchy frame and round head. The men grasped hands.

"Minister. Savior with you."

"With you, Fellow."

Idris nodded at Maryja and she hurried inside.

"I loathe this time of year. All my senses—" Idris sneezed. "Is supper almost ready?" He marched into the dining room, shooting Maryja an aggravated look she pretended not to notice.

"'The shameless women were turned by the Savior to heifers, to live out the rest of their days as dull beasts; but those with shame feared the Savior and were spared.'" said Alexei to the air, following closely behind.

Maryja paid little attention to them, chopping two carrots and dumping them into the stew on the silver platter alongside the tea, bread, and butter. Dropping the knife into the soapy sink, her hair and face— browned, limp, moist— bore through the water at the audience below, awaiting her arrival.

The Ministry's stance was that woman was her body; that whatever she was worth was to be expressed through her body, inherently sin; her only hope of redemption, lifelong servitude as a Servile, of banal household chores and rearing children. But though Maryja had put her hands together and gone through the rituals, none of the teachings had ever really sunk in.

With a soft whir her body had done what was demanded of it, allowing her to be with the plays from behind the white willow's veil.

"For the holiday party, we'll need at least twenty. She's good at ordering the others around—"

Maryja set the tray on the table, Idris closely observing.

"Fellow, ask the Savior's forgiveness if it's as bad as last week's."

Alexei bowed his head, his face nearly in his bowl like a cat lapping milk. "Dear Savior, ever watchful, make us worthy of your defense, and in your infinite wisdom, guide us through your grace into eternal bliss. Like children— from where we come and where we will return—we serve you. Amen."

"Serve you amen." As the prayer closed Idris slammed his fists, rattling the china. "Maryja! Don't you remember what the Fellow likes to drink?"

"It's a Virtue Day today, Minister. There's no drinking permitted for Godfellows," the Fellow sighed.

"Dammit, really?" Idris looked to Maryja from the priest. "Well, get some for me then."

Maryja turned but he pulled her back. "I can't drink if the Fellow isn't. Alexei, be lucky you suffer not a woman. Be so lucky." He crossed his arms, sulking.

When Alexei finished his supper the men retired to the study. Quivering from holding her laughter, Maryja rushed to her quarters in the basement, behind Idris's wines and ferments of things she'd grown, now soaking bored and useless. Collapsing on the cold paneled floor she writhed in a fit of hysterics.

A small sinuous thing, also browned, squeezed in through a gap in the wood. Sometimes worms entered through here, but she could tell this one was different, that it had some intention or direction the others did not. Maryja watched its focused wriggle, steering it closer, then away again. It soon evaded her, intriguing her with its cool intelligence.

Maryja followed it across the basement until it slid under the crack of the locked door opposite her own. She remembered the way they moved— her laughter died. It was not a worm.

When Maryja was a girl, the Ministry had condemned snakes as corrupters of women and proceeded to exterminate them. Most were burned in large, slithering piles, in the square of every city and town in the eastern and central parts of the Continent. For five months a thick layer of smoke weaved up the stratum, dulling the light, raining ashen flakes back down to earth.

Heading to the park one afternoon, she found it decimated, men in black masks torching a mound of hisses, flames so high she thought they'd burn a hole through the sky and return to the sun. Enraptured, Marija jumped back, startled by three bigger girls from her panelák. Screaming with the righteous joy of their captors:

"Had! Had! Had!";

shoving their straw dolls in her face, they hissed at her as they danced at the park's edges, jumping over little bits of debris on fire, laughing harder as Marija ran home. Fat, hot tears stung her eyes and face more than the smoke.

Returning later that night, black field against a black sky, she thought she saw something flitting across into a flat building nearby. It was impossible to tell.

Bells and Bodies

The tinny bell atop the stairs whined for Maryja's return. Shaking the sawdust from her hair she ascended to the porch with Idris's after-supper tray. The Fellow had already left to groom and ready himself for the day's final service in the Hall of the Savior. Worship songs ever simplified, the flock forgot all else in that cradling womb light, reflecting the blue godhead behind the Ministry.

Back in his chair, Idris blew smoke into the ether, mindlessly scratching the hairs on his chin. Maryja kneeled. She bowed her head into her chest as she drew herself between his legs, her forehead inches from his groin. The stench of moist skin and cloth forced its way past her closed lips, filling her mouth. She breathed as little as possible through her nostrils, spine curled. The routine was always the same, every evening when Idris was done with his supper and had nothing left to do but stare out into the sunset.

At fifty-five, Idris was now an established gentleman, a high-ranking Minister of the Justice with two cars, his own house, and one remaining Servile. Most Ministers had at least three to five. Over the years Maryja watched them come and go; some dying in childbirth, the rest sent to lower-ranking men when they produced girls instead of boys. Being the bearer of his only son Maryja was Idris's favorite, treating her with deference compared to the others.

At times Maryja tried to win the affections of the younger Serviles with little favors— bringing them sweets from the study, making them dried bouquets, to hang above their beds— but Mrs. Schopenhauer, and later, Idris, picked at any solidarity amongst the Serviles, until there was none left.

Visiting colleagues complained that Maryja was a poor housekeeper; a worse cook; too old to bear any more children. Idris said he was always keeping an eye out for a young Servile— the right one, one he felt sure would give him another male progeny. In the meantime, he kept to other men. He had little tolerance for the presence of women, who always managed to do something his mother would have disapproved of.

Maryja had been beholden to Idris since she was thirteen and he was twenty-one. Three months into her service she began to bleed, coagulations snaking from her in a black-red trail. Sneaking into Idris's father's medical volumes, the animal process of female pubescence was laid out logically, anatomical drawings neat and precise. But the experience felt not sterile but savage; pulsating pains in her groin; the insatiability for touch, spit, pink flesh; and the gore all over her once-pristine nightgown were less like a surgeon's cut and more like metallic-trapped prey yet yearning for its mate.

She did take comfort in knowing she wasn't alone, that all her sex shared in this primordial cycle with her. Such clandestine knowledge didn't have to be sacrificed to the Savior, giving her power, the only she had in the world of the Ministry.

But it came without a moment of rest. Hovering above Maryja hunched over in pain, scrubbing her underwear in the dark of the morning— drawn by the smell of the blood— Mrs. Schopenhauer scooped the girl up in her too-long talons, sealing her off in her room for a week before squawking her into Idris's bedroom, feeding the prey to her young.

Maryja's body handled Idris on its own. She knew being there would only make things worse. She recalled her favorite scenes the woman and girl put on for the house cats and stuffed animals. Weighed down not by his body but by the density of words, she felt lucky to be their receptacle. Watching something on a stage that was not hers, there was just the slight surge of her stomach, sibilants sounding from the soil.

Upon her impregnation, Maryja took up more space than she ever had. For months she tried the door, the drawers and dressers, everything she wanted locked away. Pacing, pulling, pushing, she moved, in wake and sleep. Her only company was a small, glazed portrait above the bed, of the pretty blonde Servile that preceded her. Its bovine stare tunneled into her, following her across the room or to the bath. She stared back, finding nothing to give their captivity meaning.

And there was the same dream that plagued her nearly every night, pastoral creatures moldering in open graves.

The blonde had too given birth, to a female child, both gone not long before Maryja was promised to the household. She and the Servile met once, during Maryja's first visit. The girl was silent until they were alone. She clutched her swollen belly, anticipating Idris or his mother at any moment.

"Yes, I do wish it. I can't wait for it! It's my only joy in life— yes! — my only joy, the only thing I ever wanted, the only thing that's mine— how could I not? It's sacred, what we do. Soon, it will be me. I will lay our souls at the Savior's feet, and we will be rewarded."

Over the months the organism grew, thrashing against Maryja, resenting every moment it had to spend within her walls. She imagined a violent birth, a shapeless thing consuming Idris, his family, and finally, her. Its arrival was not much tamer. Starting as a dull burning in her lower extremities like climbing a hill— fissuring skin, great push after great push— taking many bleeding, prolapsed hours to get further, only to fall back and start over again. She tried to contract into the safe vantage of the garden again, letting her body continue in the distance, but the searing called her to tear until everything had been expelled.

The constant cries of the newborn creature— rising, falling, rising— pulled Maryja out from inside herself. Nearly forgetting the exertion upon her by a culture of men, the incongruity lasted a moment too long, crushing everything. The devastation left nothing but a flattened expanse stretched on indefinitely, where she once stood. Devoid of feeling and expression— unable to recognize parts of her body as separate from tables, chairs, walls— she was left alone to stew in motherly bliss, alongside her predecessor.

For eighteen years Maryja tended to Idris and his son, mostly obediently. Despite everything, she never openly defied the Schopenhauers. Such actors, their deeds recorded, were hung from the white Weeping Tree in the Centre. So she stayed as twilight rose against her back, not stirring to satisfy an itch.

Tonight she would get in his good graces— he had asked the Fellow to intercede with the Savior on her behalf, which he only did when he was in a better mood. Perhaps she would join her companions in their revelries, play-acting eternal in the midsummer sun. They, the snakes, were real enough.

With secret knowledge once more, she smiled. She knew when to get up to take the tray away. Her body was yet a mother's, lying in wait.

In This House

Steam from the steel spout stung Maryja's face as she pumped the water for Idris's bath. When it reached the brim she stirred in lavender oil, extracted from the pitiful garden behind the house. Every spring Maryja looked on uselessly as young Serviles in white aprons and gloves sliced the just-blooming flower's tender necks, ripping out the petals, stuffing them into their front pockets and discarding the buds.

They brought the petals to their master's shop, the lavender pressed for every drop it could give before it too was discarded. A week later, the Serviles would return with vials filled with the sweet liquid that Maryja would then store on the shelf outside her door, the cycle continuing till the season's end.

Maryja imagined pastels floating gently across the tub, how soft they would feel against her work-worn skin. The last of the vegetables had sprouted five years ago, the soil no longer suitable for planting as the earth heated. But the lavender always came back— and each year it was taken before she had the chance to tend to it, to guide it towards the sun.

The door thrust open. Idris undressed, tossing his clothes aside as he sunk in, belly protruding over the oil and water, separating onto the floor. Maryja sat by his head, occasionally stirring around the edges.

"Werner is coming to visit tomorrow. He finally got promoted— Under-Secretary— next, it's Secretary, then Vice Prime." He sighed, sinking back. "Come. We'll save it for later."

Idris's son lived in a nearby province, following the same trajectory in the Justice as his father, from what Maryja had gathered from bits of the men's conversations. What the differences were in each role remained a mystery, but with promotions came more of everything. She pictured the boy, flippant and bored of mastering households, deviants, women. Papers stamped, endlessly shuffled around, the Ministry constantly expanded, gestated for its own sake.

Thinking of him made her scratch herself furiously. Idris loved his son dearly, never refusing him anything.

"When Alexei was going on about the ceremony— I don't recall the last time you asked me for another woman. Or maybe you did, and it slipped my mind," Idris laughed. "Women are usually persistent about such matters."

Maryja remained taciturn, wary of what imploring reached the surface, crying out loud. In what situations had she begged— in this house; in black rooms, bare light burning long enough to singe the pleading from her throat, her welled eyes dried to lifelessness. Much of it had all been for that delicate, nervous girl, in the early days, her only intimate friend.

They loved the lavender, their lives buried in the bushels.

'From you, I have been absent—' and other mindless poetic risks worth the song of the words Maryja and her lover memorized, scrambling sounds on the tips of their tongues, the roofs of their mouths reconstructed in new forms of expression, just for them. Their bodies tangled like roots, traversing lips and fingertips in foreign territories cultivated and made home. Another orphaned young, her lover was not long in the wilderness before the Ministry hounded her down too.

In her doe eyes Maryja found an eternity of natural lush, filled with as many cottages and gardens and plays as they could conjure. It was the endless hills beyond the linear world, the true faces behind the roles of Serviles, Ministers, Under-Secretaries, Fellows. There also youthful plans blossomed, pushed up from the tiny cracks in the Ministry's concrete.

But as the range of the Eye expanded, their flora and fauna struggled to grow, hope shortening like days.

In one last attempt at green, they made it outside the city proper, dewy lunar grass prickling their feet. It hurried them, prancing towards the metal fence a few meters ahead, pulled down either side to a fine point. But before Maryja could hoist the waify girl over, She— mother of the Ministry, watching, splitting herself like mitosis— deployed many copies of black armor to trample their last seed of hereafter.

After the girl was sent away both men and Serviles grew tiresome to Maryja. The only other person she'd ever loved had also drifted up in grey flakes, landing nowhere but dreams. Maryja tried not to think of those happy sunny days, for fear of souring Idris's placid mood. She existed like the jars in the basement, fermenting those never to be seen again.

Since then, Idris's mother forbade Maryja from sullying the lavender. The matron never failed to catch wind of Maryja nearing, scanning overhead for Maryja's presence in the garden.

She couldn't stop scratching, the sensation growing stronger.

"Maybe you'd relish the company. But maybe not— you're always off in your little head. Maybe you'd turn them against me. Mother used to warn me of that. Even Werner— I like too much being a god in his eyes.

But there's something about you. Your stench— I've always been given to strange propensities. It is the smell of that which my family has built over generations, that shaped our Ministry and this new world we've carved out for ourselves. The Serviles embody what we've been working toward, through their toil and service. But only you capture this distinction between us so perfectly."

Soaping his shiny head, he grabbed her hand, dragging it under the surface.

"Bring some more oil from the basement and make yourself clean by me."

Maryja curtseyed and left the bathroom. She lingered in the perfume that permeated the hallway as impotent rage overflowed. She had grown used to his hateful embrace, but never to being chided for that which she had not chosen, severed from all futures. It made her want to burst forth, the onus on her to remain a body.

She was compressed ever tighter into the house— head bashing against the ceiling, feet sucked beneath the floors, hips pressed into the walls, moving with her curvature. She no longer existed anywhere else; even the backyard, a distant dream.

There were only two vials left. Maryja stepped on something squishy. The brownish snake darted into the locked room again before she could catch it. She pressed her ear to the door, now warm.

A great war march stormed on. A woman screamed against commands hatefully precise; something cried for its mother, and a body slammed against the other side, forcing the door ajar. Maryja froze, eyes leaking. Blinded by the rush of sunlight, she parted the veil of the willow tree from her face.

A long, viscous black snake emerged from the pond and settled at the tree's roots. Raising its neck, it sucked its tail up rapidly into its unhinged jaw in an infinite spiral. Maryja instinctually recoiled back into the cold room again. But beneath the floor was still earth, and beneath that, the cutting scent of something being exhumed.

The tinny bell had been chiming unanswered. Idris barged in, nude and huffing like an angry baby. The obsidian creature had followed Maryja back to the world of the Ministry, slunk in the farthest corner.

"How did you get in here? How?!" Idris cried. "Mother always kept it locked!"

Idris threw a vial at Maryja, striking her pelvis. She tried to stand but slipped across the glittering shards, bloodied oil slick as snakeskin. Idris hoisted her up against the door, splaying her arms. He pulled a piece of glass from her rib as she quivered with dry tears. Many tiny tongues were flickering around them. Bodies black, brown, and striped sprung from the ophidian mother as he smeared the mixture on her face.

"She's purified!" Idris laughed madly.

The snakes dispersed as Idris chased Maryja upstairs. The richness of lavender, mold, and fetid meat forced her into an impasse. Her loins burned more fiercely than they had in years; she was now on the front against the rabid copulation. Just before he peaked, a force threw him from atop her. His head hit the bedpost, dropping him to the floor. Maryja heaved.

Everything was silent but for a low, steady ticking. Hands of hours and minutes moved unperturbed over his lumbering body. Despite their exercise from the world, the snakes had survived. So she gathered all the lost time in her arms, bearing it down upon him and letting it strike. Scattered around, the jumbled numerals encircled him.

The bath was still steamy; the oil cooled her itch a little. Maryja soaked in it, picking out the last of the shards, the water made murky by filth and fluids. When she finished she checked that he was still still, no longer thinking of him.

Maryja stood before the new bloom resting in the dark, cloying inhale, exhale. Ready to cross the border to touch, a cold light washed over. Affixed to the Hall spire— gothic, electronic, brooding— She saw everything. Laser-blue, metallic pupil homing in, all in Her light was absorbed into that flattened expanse, space enough for the memory of every transgression committed by the Ministry.

One day, that gaze would flush, casting sinners into the pits below; then the lavender would be hers, to have and to hold.

The Mother Approaches

Maryja ducked under the bush, digging until her dirt-caked fingernails brushed against love poems and letters long buried. Pages signed 'AM' were interspersed with images of Maryja naked in the bathtub, flailing her legs in delight; of her on Idris's bed, breasts exposed, head thrown back in laughter; of her and her lover, kissing in the bush, blue dresses crumpled at their feet.

Beneath the sensual were a trio of news clippings, Maryja reading and re-reading them under the watchful light. It was the first time in years she'd seen that face outside her dreams. Even in the colorless print— struggle, defeat, victory— Maryja could feel her red hair burning through the factual lies of who, what, when, where, and why, as reported by the Ministry. She still felt her mother was somewhere beyond its reach.

As the first birds heralded the black hour morphing blue, she stuck everything in her pocket, retreating inside.

A silver dark had split Idris's prostrated body in half. Maryja pulled the leaden comforter over him, guiltless as a sleeping babe. She closed the drapes and the door behind her before descending. Pulling the string, flies mottled the bulb of the basement light.

More varicolored bodies frenzied in from underground. Maryja slid on the slimy lumps, warm guts sticking to her dress and face. The pain in her stomach and groin surfaced again as the lukewarm numb of the bath dissipated. The snakes wormed their way into her bed and dresser— the yellowed book under the floorboard beneath her shoes, eating its pages. She wrestled from them whatever was left, crumbling in her hands.

In anger she stomped her foot down, nearly killing one; the damage to its back reflected in her own as a sharp stabbing pain.

Maryja watched as they consumed the one photo of her with the Schopenhauers; the flimsy icon of the Savior, gifted to all Serviles who bore male children; and the garb from her betrothal ceremony— blue, white, and red, of the flag of what was her country. The only thing they hadn't gotten to were what was in her pocket.

Barraging through the door, knocking down the fermented jars, they made their way into the house. Some headed to the backyard, while others, led by the brownish one, went for the bedrooms. She followed, standing at the threshold of Idris's room, shed scales trailing out of his bureau.

The mother approached— jaw unhinged— swallowing Maryja down the pungent walls of an eternal tube. As the children had consumed her Servile life, the mother consumed the pain of her Servile body and spirit, metabolizing it into the flesh network. Fecund membranes suspended her newborn form in an amniotic sac. A pulsing propulsion grew more powerful, pushing her out from the humid comfort. Opening her eyes again, Marija was thrust from a woman into a scream, pained breath enveloped in sweetness.

Jana peered out the second-story window. Her neighbor darted her head around, spotting her while taking out her refuse, giving Jana a mocking smile. She was middle-aged, with beady eyes and a long tail of hair whipping down her back. Attending one of Jana's plays not a week ago, she now donned a silver Eye patch, the kind given to Ministry informants. Scurrying over to a group of soldiers— weapons hipped at the ready— they slowed their walk, looking in the same direction as the neighbor.

One of the men never took his eyes off Jana until they had disappeared past the end of the road. She panted, her shaky hands almost not dialing.

"Švanda Theatre."

"It's Jana. Get Matěj."

Jana felt the bored operator perk up. The phone was set on the table with a quick slam, feet scurrying from the booth. A cigaretted voice picked up a minute later.

"Jana, you're late again—"

"Tell Mother I need my *kroj*. Matěj, please send for me the white *kroj*."

Matěj silently nodded. "Everything's ready." He paused. "Give my love to the little one."

Jana dressed, wrapping the dozing infant in a shawl around her chest, waiting until the neighbor's lights went out before leaving.

The houses grew wider and further apart as Jana walked with her baby down the quiet country road. She knew which roads were closed after the shows ended, which had checkpoints and which didn't. She took a shortcut through the wood, that the occupiers were too afraid of going into it to catch her. Here amongst the moss and mushrooms was where she first played pretend, long before she became a real actress.

Being onstage for over a decade, Jana had grown accustomed to having eyes on her, both admiring and strange. But she was beginning to cave under the constant pressure of this kind of observation, that waited greedily for any slight, or even the perception of one. Two other actresses and one of the theatre's seamstresses had been taken from their homes in the past three months, for failing to report their menstrual cycles. While two of them were returned and made to retire, her pregnant friend, a decorated screen actress, Jana never saw again.

Though she'd managed to keep her occupation thus far, she could no longer fully immerse herself in another world, when so fragile a thing was at danger in this one.

Marija had been mostly quiet. When sunset ripened to twilight she looked up, the reflection of so many stars, each tiny spotlights in her purple eyes. Jana knew her girl was destined for something incredible; if she had somewhere her own to grow into.

In the open field, the world felt briefly sure, like the protection of a womb. Rumbling divine headlights shone from the distance, slowly illuminating them. Jana pressed Marija to her protective breast, calm sway pacifying her to sleep.

Cries In Her Flesh

From a dream of stars and cradled notes Maryja awoke, wary of why the bell rang. She eventually headed upstairs with breakfast. The spired Eye peeked out from the slightly opened curtains. Idris was sullen as she laid the tray beside him. His arm rested on it, but he did not eat. His face was turned up towards the blonde portrait, his eyes blank. The clock had stopped ticking.

Two swollen red lumps burst out from Idris's slippers. With a smile, Maryja thought he looked more bloated than usual. Little snakes traversed the room, their cries reverberating in her flesh. More poured out of the walls— from under pictures and cloth, slithering over Idris unawares, clinging to his legs as they would a father's. The brownish one emerged from his gaping mouth, darker against the white trim of his robe.

Maryja staggered back, bringing down another painting, of Idris's son, behind her.

"What's that?!" Idris shot up, hocking phlegm onto his plate. He rubbed his head, letting out a small puppy-whine, but there was just a spot of red. He put the tray aside and pulled a shirt from the bureau.

"Werner's already waiting for me. It's Friday— Praise Day. We must tell of our love for the Savior, so on and so on— we'll go somewhere to dine while they all suckle the teat." Idris laughed. "Does my blasphemy offend you? It's not my mother, after all. I'm a Minister. Nothing changes that."

"Snakes—"

"Snakes? There?" He looked down, lifting each foot. A snake cried out as he caved its head in with his heel.

A knifing pain sliced through the left side of Maryja's head, behind her eye. She clutched herself. Idris laughed.

"Yes, the snakes. I keep them in the basement, in the other room. Surprised it took you so long to notice. They've been under your nose the whole time. You thought they were all killed, but I spared them. I'm their god too!"

The brownish snake followed his howl into the bath. Maryja heard the water run, plops diving under the surface. Idris would soon disappear outside, a small part of things unknowable to all but She, recording. Anything could change on a whim, but at least he had chosen it.

Streaming sunlight softened the starkness of the Eye, making the harsh lines and the order of everything more opaque. There were the usual passings, straggling Ministers and black trucks making their morning rounds, when suddenly a white van quickly drove by, screeching around the corner.

Inside, Marija looked up from her mother's face to the flashing, spinning world quickly left behind as they sped ahead. Only a few shapes didn't stretch out or above in the blur of black-yellow; neon blues and reds, flashing; gray blocks, that blended into the landscape, almost invisible, the deep verdure followed once more by dark sky and ground.

At places between muted and vibrant shades were little piles of hot orange, fed little squares by figures circled and clapping, like when her mother hid her face and reappeared again, silly and the sum of everything.

"They've added our plays to the list," Jana whispered. "But I have copies."

In the colored conflagration Marija fell back into sleep; when her big baby eyes fluttered open again it was into daylight. Bright smells of flowers and grass and fresh air permeated her nose and mouth. She sneezed; Jana wiped her nose, nodding to the rumbling white carriage as it took off.

There was a little home for them, tucked away in the country's eastern valley, bordered by nature, without Eyes and the men attached to them.

"We're safe. Shutting the problems of the world behind us—"

"I remember. Close to my mother's."

Maryja was alone once more; tearing, she sneezed again. The bovine eyes witnessed the whole scene, withholding judgement. They didn't move from Maryja wherever she went. Maryja stared back, also not averting her gaze.

"Your name is Bojana."

The rosy-cheeked visage jumped to the floor, landing in front of the bureau.

The opacity softened more, the room fluid and malleable. The walls were smooth and a little damp, the floors coming in and out as a tide. A chorus of women, their cries of pleasure, moaned from inside the walls. Maryja felt a rush of blood move below her belly. One of the voices belonged to she whom couldn't speak again, that Maryja was more than surprised to hear. The young woman's warm phantom touch pulled her dress up, peeling her undergarments off, steady reaching into folded depths.

The house wracked back and forth; Maryja fell onto the bed, moving with the creaking rhythm. Vigorously, their widening came together in a gush, hunger desperately gorging itself until satiated.

A Grave

Maryja was meant to prepare Werner's room for his visit. It was mostly as he'd left it; everything in its right place, overlooking her once fruitful garden. As a boy, he'd cry and pound his little fists against her legs whenever she came in to change the sheets or sweep. It gave her a similar aching as Idris's bedroom, worse when he was away on Ministry trips. Once, when the boy was eight, she tried to wrestle him down from the window and he fell, turning red and black and blue under his shirt. Turning over in the mud, wincing, the first few moments of silence almost sprouted hope.

But when his father returned, Werner said nothing of it. From then until he left home, he gave commands to the air, never directly asking her for anything.

The negation compounded like stones stacked on her chest until she couldn't be in Werner's presence without feeling she would disintegrate. Calling 'Maryja, Maryja!'—looking right through her— the game extended over ever longer periods, much to the amusement of Idris and his guests. It was then that her skin first crawled with the insatiable desire to shed.

For as long as Werner lived there she avoided her reflection, fearing she had scratched off what face she once had, body pared, ceasing to exist. He would often pace around the kitchen while she prepared the meals, wooing her name like a spirit unacknowledged but felt, a sensation or presence not fully formed. Whatever she did or didn't do had no effect on the boy's trajectory; he continued to move through his schooling, into university, finally siphoned off into the Justice as a young man.

She had given birth to him, but she was not his mother.

There were too many of the limbless things now, in every vexing corner of the house, eating Idris's leftovers and whatever was in the pantry. There were over a hundred— maybe a thousand. It was impossible to tell and too much to fight. But as none of them took notice of her, she decided to take another bath. Placing the other's portrait across from her she let herself sink, dreams and memories collapsing in on each other until the two were indistinguishable, sucked deep into the primordial past.

Marija was spread out on the floor beside the cats, basking in the sun-soaked living room. Pulling herself up to the window, she noticed that the strange woman who liked to watch them from the willow wasn't there today. Her mother was still upstairs as the man rested on the chaise, snoring like a breeze.

Staring up at him, she put her ear close to his lips, pinching his nose until a rush of air blew out of his mouth. He wasn't particularly familiar, but it wasn't the first time she'd seen someone like him napping in the high summer afternoon, satisfied and spent.

Jana came down in a mellifluous trill: *'and everyone reaps what they sow—'*. Twirling around, she finished the song with a dramatic fall onto the couch. Under the cover of her dress draped over him, she threw his arm around her waist, kissing Marija's forehead. From the cascading firefalls washing over her, Marija poked her mother's breast and they all laughed.

Once they dozed off, Marija ventured outside. Beneath the fragrant sweet of the flowers was a hint of acridity. She thought little of it at first, playing as usual, but it wouldn't go away. She checked for something dead, sometimes found curled up or splayed by the pond; there was nothing.

It was emanating the vegetable plot. She didn't understand; never had anything gone wrong here. Poppies had popped up between the necrosing green-red-purple; over the thin wire fence she could see the ground concaving. The hole only grew the more furiously she tried to fill it. Finally, it collapsed.

Parasitic creatures fed off what was once a cow and her calf, the black-white mold in the same fuzzy pattern as their spotted roan.

The sky closed to a speck as Marija descended. Any air was vacuumed out by the grave heart of the garden, trapped in the rigor mortis rot. The limb of the mother had decayed over its yearling, trying to shield it from the blunt force cracked across their skulls. Their clouded gazes followed Marija as wriggling digits crept in and out of their soft punctures. The bodies bloated with her anxiety, making her yet more anxious, the space between them narrowing.

Echoes of whinnied pleading leaked from dirt and carcass; Marija's tongue soured, death and pink livid flesh melding into one briefly resurrected beast, just long enough for some inhuman cry— expelled power of powerlessness— to jolt from her throat, followed by the pitiful, terrified expulsion of its violently dying child.

Turning her face to the last of the sun, it was blotted by a black ring. The snake tunneled down, swallowing the dead. It slowed down, letting Marija approach. Its yellow eyes, relaxed and patient, didn't meet hers directly. Air leaked in from on high; with a deep breath she filled up her stomach and chest.

Wrapping herself tightly around its glossy scales she rode it to the surface.

Circling the pond, the snake shed its skin. The cold stench clung to Marija, vigorously scrubbing her limbs and face. As the dirt sunk the sky opened, though an invisible dread lingered overhead, threatening to clamp down at any moment. The chill had spread into the roots of everything; the flowers, grass, and willow, duller, stiffer. She almost wished the maggots had consumed her as well— it was just by chance that the mother and child were in the pit, and not her.

"Hello, Marija? Are you out there? Bring in some tomatoes, won't you?" Jana sang.

But none were ripe. Marija raced back inside, the house now Schopenhauer again. The young girl lingered in the tepid bath as the water drained. Flecks of dirt stuck to Maryja as she dressed.

The front door opened; a man called out from the foyer.

"Hello, Maryja? Are you there?"

Idris would never consider that Maryja could be anywhere besides there, waiting for his command. She peered over the railing where he couldn't see her. Werner was tall and a little unsure, most of his childish piggishness gone. He was even smiling. Fat hot droplets from her hair dripped down her dress, puddling at the top of the stairs. He came halfway up, calling out to her again.

"I'm glad to see you." His expression was full of pity. "Father said you saw a snake? How odd— I thought they were extinct." He paused, lowering his voice and head. "I don't know what to say for myself."

Maryja began clawing her arm. "They're coming from the basement. They ate everything—"

"Don't worry about that. But— won't you come downstairs, and we'll look?"

She turned from him.

"Stay there. I'll look."

Passing the study where the men plotted Werner walked down the hall into the kitchen. With her back to the wall, she listened for sibilates between his paces. She wished he would leave.

"I didn't see anything there. I don't think I've ever seen a real snake before," he chuckled. "It would probably frighten me." He stepped onto the landing.

"There's a place I heard about at the Justice, Maryja, for you to retire." Werner approached slowly, as though come upon something feral. "It's in the country, with a garden, like the one you had when I was a boy. You could be happy there. There are Fellows there, that help women like you."

He held his hand out to her.

"I know you've suffered— won't you trust me? I'm not my father; I'm not blind to his faults. You wouldn't have to come back here, if that's what you wished. Please, let me help you. It would ease my mind—"

Maryja raised her head to face him, her body shaking from the pressure. He was a little weepy— he usually was toward the end of one of his games. He always gave a spectacular finish; he might have made a fine player for a scene in the garden. One last joke, to finally wipe her from existence, just for the fun of it.

"I used to call for you, and you would never answer— but I hardly imagined that one day I might call out your name, and you wouldn't be there. I always thought of you as a part of this house, as home. What would this place be, without you?

But I just got promoted, see?" Werner pulled the collar of his jacket from which a pin beamed, like Idris's. "I have influence now. Father's got old rivals in the Tribunal, so he can't do it.

I know that we've hurt each other. Things were, overwrought. But I'd like the chance to make up for lost time. Please?"

The glowing warmth illuminated the rifts mottled through the flattened expanse. Rising from the earth was the outline of a domed tree in the distance.

"We'll go to the Justice, and they'll help us—"

The possibility of hope eroded what was left of being, escaping from Maryja like vapor. Innards turned to ash, the intense release liquifying muscle and bone. For the first time since she'd been in the Schopenhauer household, she felt as if she really were nothing more than a pathetic aching beast.

"Maryja, are you alright?! Maryja! Maryja—"

She knew they would take her wherever they wanted; her consent was not required. That terrible dark light shone upon her, in all her failure and shame, wrenched from the garden like a weed. Convulsions made her fluid body squirm towards what was nearest. Her flopping hands tried grabbing the door, handle hot against her cooling skin.

An audience watched Maryja flailing Idris's suits from the bureau, falling in on its back until a hollow echo rang. There dilated the path to putrefaction, where the odious vapor had begun breaking down corporeal structures of existence. Rooted beyond sense, petrified in child-like ignorance was the malice inflicted on the women's bodies, their pride and innermost sanctities. Tendrils of fear lashed at her, to drag her to where even snakes could not reach.

Belly to the ground, each stair gnashing her head crushed ophidian bodies, pulp not softening the blows. Girlish screams called from the depths like sirens, erections from her nightmares threatening to crystalize at any moment. Softened limbs spasming slipped on in thoughtless panic.

Into The Abyss

Dreamlike, the garden stirred slightly. It appeared as it always had, but dread still lingered in the stratum and her gut. In the floodlight of the full moon Marija tiptoed to her mother's room, pressing her ear to the door. It was warm with the crackling of the hearth.

"I need you to—yes, I'm sure, they found it— I don't know, maybe it was him, or someone else saw us— no, I didn't say anything! I need money to survive Matěj, how else can I take care of— well, can you get us out? Can you call them again? We're going in the morning then, to get her out of here—"

Marija ran downstairs, heavy breaths flinging her out the back door. The urge to keep moving— the sharpness of her senses— were drowned out by the lavender. No longer her mother, but just a voice, too distant to be urgent:

"Come back into the house, Marija! Marija's out in the garden— they might see her, Matěj, what if they see her? I can't hide her here anymore! Can't you—"

Marija fell to her knees by the pond. The nocturne quiet was fissured by engined growls through the gravel road that led to the house. A false brightness outshone the illusory safety of lunation, the blinding stinging the watery surface. Curt static unintelligible looped in between the heavy-wheeled rotations.

Searching for reflected yellow, dark sheen, in the black against black against black, it was difficult to see anything of protection. *Maybe it delivered me to them*, Marija thought; *maybe it only saved me for something else.*

'*Had, had, had—*'

Marija finally looked to Jana calling for her, to escape through yet another tunnel, out the front door to another road, but she could see in the pond that it too was touched by the light. She went back upstairs, to her mother's voice and arms, but Jana pushed the girl into her own bedroom and locked the door. Marija pulled and screamed, but there was no answer.

Black uniforms black-masked barreled in from behind the tree, making their way toward the house.

Boots stormed up the stairs. Men gave commands, dragging Marija out into the hallway, torches pointed. Jana was naked before the roaring hearth, her hair indistinguishable from flames spinning forked shadows on the walls. Her limbs, that ran from house to house to protect her daughter, moved gracefully, evading the muscled clumps seeking to capture them.

Yet Jana was hardly aware of them or anything else. Celebrating the fall back into the abyss, she could not be put down any other way, taking all of life with her.

The unit tied her mother to the bedposts with quick mechanical efficiency. The fire revved into action accompanied her divine laughter, a sour vapor of burnt flesh with that of the balmy flowers untouched on her nightstand. Ashes fell in elongated shapes, taking on a slickness from the oil of the torches. Marija sobbed back to her room as they finished off the raging maternal body, its thundering cry omnipotent.

More incinerators had spread their flame—from the vegetable plot to the lavender borders in the wilder, the reeds around the pond and the willow, silvery glow choking on the smoke. Hoisting herself out the window, an icy grip caught Marija's ankle. She kicked it away, balancing along the ledge of the roof.

A bird's dirge cut through the last of the lingering blaze. Her mother coated the air, thicker than the blanketed drifts now covering what was their home. Marija jumped, weightless, suspended by Jana alone. But the male appendages found her again, binding her hands and throwing a black hood over her head. The harder she writhed, the tighter the grip.

Below the watery surface the audience watched, its patience finally rewarded.

Many Blue Coats

It had been years since Maryja had been to the Centre, and longer since the Justice. The pavement was scattered with pinkish spring leaves now wilting. Behind her, a compression of arbored browns and greens rolled on in the distance, tattered grey above barely hinting at the glint of metal slicing the landscape.

Through the sulfurous haze, she could see children, chasing one another and laughing; friends and lovers, arms linked, wandering. There was no Ministry there, only the sun. Werner hurried her away before she could get a closer look.

Each house in the Justice Minister's district was identical, branded with the same emblem of the Eye. The streets all led to the four great structures of the city, that overlooked the white Weeping Tree. Knotted and twisted and unlike the precision of everything around it, it was kept as a reminder, that their domination was over all of life.

The buildings made them and everyone they passed on the street— Ministry men; black-clad men, watching; schoolboys on their way home, one shouting 'Boo!' at her, much to the amusement of his classmates— as ants in comparison. Concrete, geometrical, incurvated in impossible shapes, the three Ministries stood side by side opposite the hive-like Hall of the Savior, crowned in a stained-glass depiction of a domed tree topped by a bloody sun, flanked by two white birds.

"Werner!" A tall man with a white bird in flight on his breast pocket, a discolored splotch on his face, shook Werner's hand. "Your Minister must have been pleased with the initiative."

"Hans! Yes, everything's following projections." Werner smiled proudly.

"How's Minister Schopenhauer then? Still in Extractions?"

"You know him, they'll have to drag him out of there when the time comes."

"The old dog," Hans laughed.

Werner's voice lowered. "I read the Info this morning. You've done a magnificent job of cleaning everything up." He grimaced. "Agitator. How could he? He was with us from the beginning. But he was always, sentimental. Father thought so too. He's in the Savior's hands now."

Maryja kept her gaze on the two hung fools gently swaying from the Tree. Hans peered over to the last building on the right. His head reached the high branches, as though to bite the bloom just showing itself.

"The Libers are conscripting him. Probably to the enemy colonies. Let those lawless Yank apes deal with it."

From behind the Tree the red-haired woman appeared, dressed in a gold-lined frock. She smiled, skipping on the path to the Justice. No one else seemed to notice her. As the crowd thickened, Maryja walked a little ahead of Werner, allowing herself to be imbued with the image of shedding this drudgery, fitted with a new life that was her own. She tried not to become too intoxicated by it, but the woman's joy and free movement made it hard to be completely unaffected by the possibility of renewal.

Werner nodded to himself, tinkering with his pin to capture the radiant midday beams. "I need to get approval from the Retirement Office, before I can get stamped by the Pre-Trial Commission— no, wait! I'm forgetting something— dammit! We'll have to stop at the Servile office— those bastards have to sign off on it first—"

Endless lines wound outside the many offices, shuffling feet dispirited. Serious-suited men quickly darted from one open, closed door to another, pollinating with what papers they carried. The low buzz of fluorescent aggravation and backtracking quietly filled the floor, all unsure if they were where they were supposed to be. Low ceilings and gray windings compacted the space.

Maryja followed Werner as he argued with tired middle-aged men for stamps and signatures, threatening them with his father until they complied. Near one of the offices she spotted the woman in a section that jutted over the back of the building. The window there was tight and smudged; no one had bothered to clean it or completely block it out. There was a short path from the Justice to the Liberation, overgrown with grass and weeds.

A faceless man slumped over from the shell-linked chain clasping his arms to his back was dragged from the Justice by two green-suited men. His head retreated under in defeat. She could tell he had accepted that he was going to die, in some painful way or another. She wondered if he had been a friend of her mother's or had known of her.

Moving from the window before anyone caught her, the gilded flash turned an impalpable corner, beckoning her. The hung fools looked on, to see what she would do. Following her lead, Maryja couldn't recall how she'd gotten here, and there were no signs or squeaks of shoes against polished floors to lead her back. Invisible to men the red-haired woman walked faster, following the trail of spired light into the belly of the Justice. Maryja struggled to keep up. The palpitations in her chest fell into her feet, heart-beating the laminate. A random cry would reverberate in her ear, passing, then calling her name; her actual one, correctly pronounced.

Upon turning the final corner the woman disappeared, leaving Maryja before a hidden hallway.

On either side were five doors, windowless and absorbing all sound. Facing her at the end was the womb from which serpentines leaped, squirming in the grips of the black-clad men. Thick dark skins shot up over female prey— hung from hooks like many blue coats— swallowed and tossed down a chute into oblivion. A pattern of drips sounded as from a leaky pump, and a sweet smell permeated the air.

She saw the face of one— tanned, eyes purple in the electric red glow. Thumping balled hands hit with the rhythm of the other's dangled feet, pendulumed wall to almost door, but to the same end as blue before— black bag over her too, as blue next.

The disembodied screams burrowed into Maryja, baiting that which had watched until now, finally emerging from beneath the surface.

In a stairwell guarded, she felt the sun setting on her back. Two freshly dead swung outside as she returned to where she lost Werner. She knew it was him from how he began to whine, the same as when he first escaped from her. Gripping her shoulder, he had her again.

"Wrong way," he laughed nervously.

With the papers gathered Maryja slumped in behind other greyed aprons, waiting for their hearings in an older part of the building where the Ministry first began. None of the Serviles lifted their heads— she thought that maybe they'd seen it too, that they were worried that the men and the others would think it was madness.

The one ahead of her turned, flicking her red forked tongue at Maryja before entering the darkened room.

Eventually Maryja was admitted inside. Dragged legs screeched across the floor as she sat across from two pins she'd never seen before, blue gems halving flat black ovals. Watching them watching like their Savior mother, their span expanded, inevitably alighting on something she wished to hide. It wouldn't end until they found whatever it was, whether or not it was there.

What was there was the queen of slick vulgar bodies, hissing the answers for her. Reminding her subject that that which had will could still be blistered— that the warmth of being seen could scorch and ascend far quicker than it could move without her help. She better than all knew from where the snakes had come; what to say that the men wanted to hear, to avoid being put back in the pile.

Tall doors built for gods led to the Tribunal, lit only by a plain chandelier in the center. White-robed men upon high wooden benches noticed nothing outside their files. Some were asleep. Werner sat Maryja at a chair and desk like those in pictures of the schools of before. The whispering died down as Werner approached the counselor's bench.

"Please, will you—" he said to the bailiff in an agitated voice, who passed the stamps and signatures up to a wizened man rising from his hibernation.

"Great Honorifics! Savior Be Praised! I am Under-Secretary Werner Schopenhauer. My Vice-Prime informed me that there was a spot open for a Retiree, and that I should be likely to—"

The judge grunted as he shuffled through the papers. "Where is the form from the Committee of Transfers and Patrols? Has the Minister there heard the Servile's case?"

"The, what? But I— I was told by the Serviles office that—"

"Under-Secretary, nothing gets done in a Transfers Tribunal without the signature of the Minister of the Committee of Transfers and—"

"Honorifics! Please! My father, Minister—"

"Sir, your father nothing. There are rules." The judge yawned.

A second bailiff came in from behind the judge's bench, handing him another stack of papers. The judge read to himself as others resumed side conversations. Werner opened his mouth to speak but fell silent. When the judge was finished, he conferred with the others.

"It says here that it is the recommendation of the Wardens, based upon interviews with the Servile, that she remains in your father's household. Besides, you didn't get the Transfers stamp. Perhaps if you had a Special Joint Recommendation from the Retirement office— the Tribunal must reject this request at this time. You may appeal no sooner than—"

Werner struck the desk. "Does the Savior not preach mercy? Does the Savior, whose light shines so brightly upon you all, doom all else to shadow? Damn you, old fools! Who are you to dictate the fate of all? Blasphemers— you decide not for the Savior! What of mercy— mercy?!"

The judge slowly stood, leering down at Werner and Maryja.

"Under-Secretary, what do you expect to gain from your insolence? You have no case. Waste no more of our time."

He turned to another judge, sighing. "Shall we go eat?"

The trial was adjourned, over in a quarter of an hour. Werner was removed from his station by the bailiff, sent back into the hall to make room for the next hearing. All the while a hot viscosity jetted through Maryja's veins, making her glisten, her abdomen and groin throb. That which she had imagined could have happened here leaked from her like sweat, rivering out past the desk, freezing on the cold court floors.

When they were home Werner helped Maryja upstairs, laying her down in his bed. Dragging the point of his pin across the mirror he followed it with the pull of his finger, red welling over the slash. Angrily, the bloody reflection smashed, the lavender outside resting in pieces.

"Damn that Tribunal! When I move up, I'm going to—"

"Werner," Maryja sat up. "At the Justice— I saw a red room. Do you know it?"

Werner looked away, his pink hue whitening. "I haven't heard of such—"

"There are no snakes left, are there?"

"Well, no, Maryja, I don't think there are. Don't let them trouble you anymore." Werner turned to her. "Why don't you rest here? I need to draw up an appeal—"

"If those aren't snakes, then—"

"Maryja! I don't know of everything that goes on in the Justice. It's like a machine that takes many parts to run." Werner sighed. "I'm in the mud with most of the men. Now you know."

"There's a cold light, like the Eye—"

Werner snorted, breaking into squealing laughter so hard he shook. "Lies! Those old rumors! Did someone tell you that when you wandered off? Everyone knows, everyone knows it's—"

His bleating went limp as tears turned to sobs of boyish loss and disappointment. Resting his head upon Maryja's breast, staining her dress sanguine, Werner clung immovably to her, laying her back down. He brought his face close so that their lips nearly touched.

"How could we do this, to a mother?"

The serpentine children began to gather in his room, clambering onto the bed, covering them both. The slick black undulated through her, shooting from her loins in a slimy, metallic sizzle. Little bodies spewed in all directions. They whined as their mother slithered on top of Werner, still immersed in Maryja. She bit into his neck, his eyes and skin glazing over.

Maryja remembered the venom from one of the doctor's books. It paralyzed the prey, softening sinew and bone to help break it down in the ophidian gut. With jaw unhinged, the queen took him whole, the Eye noting Maryja's helplessness to stop the creature or get up from the bed. He sank, head returned to the depths.

Her offspring cleared the way for her descent as she carried Maryja to her lair in the basement. Maryja could no longer move even her digits of her own volition. Trying to recall the garden, to draw from it, came up dry. The power was no longer hers. With no way out, the remnants of what her body endured— its laborious usage, its usefulness to the Ministry— dispersed into the ether, the house taking on her role.

The imprint of Werner gave its final struggle, his thrashes not paining her. Once in Maryja's room, the snake regurgitated his flaccid body. The hungry young attacked, feasting until only bone remained. Maryja thought his disintegration wasn't dissimilar to her own, happening outside her body instead of to it this time as the young retreated through the cracks in the floor. The brownish snake lingered beside her before following its siblings.

The queen remained, nestling into her new home.

Of Lavender Petals

Maryja woke feverish to a fury of scored skin, white flakes like snow around her bed. An uncontrollable shiver rattled her as she laced her apron, looser over her straighter hips and smooth stomach. The tinny bell rang for the second time. Yanking it from its hook, it shattered into two dissonant pieces. Sneering at it, she smiled.

"No, the Eye saw—. It was the first thing—. No, the Ministers there didn't either. Then where is he? Maryja!"

Idris stood atop the basement stairs trailed by two Fellows, one young and nervous, the other fat and red.

"Let's do this in the dining room. Maryja, we need to speak with you. Come upstairs."

As Maryja entered the kitchen the tables and chairs and the whirring oven began to peel from the yellowing-purpling walls like paper, growing or shrinking whenever she turned to look. Crouching down made her feel better, closer to the ground where the steaming pots, real or not, were out of view.

She sat to Idris's left, half-listening to the Fellows arguing, their voices distant. Idris scrunched his face in confusion, wringing his hands. Before she could reach the warmth of a bowl of leftover stew Idris snatched it away.

Maryja glared at him, but he wasn't paying attention. Her teeth ached.

"The Fellows are here on an urgent matter. It's about Werner."

"We just have a few questions," The young one tried to smile.

"Answer truthfully, Servile. The Savior is watching."

"Just tell them, Maryja. Please." Idris panted.

The red hand slammed a note on the table, the coffee rolling off, bitter flood billowing at his feet. "What do you know of this?"

"It doesn't match his handwriting, Minister. Does she know how to write? We would dread having to report this— "

The note was a rambling of indescribable beings and objects, letters dissolved to primeval symbols lashed by void beasts. Estranged from meaning, words passed the border into the Real, obscuring her path back to herself. There, the true godhead of the Ministry revealed its form— never fully— eternally burning out of her breadth. The irritation in her skin, which she tried stupidly to resist, animated into chaos. It never quite reached fulfillment, almost making sense.

"Maryja, you saw Werner this afternoon. I know he was here." Idris gestured at the note. "But he never returned home. His Vice-Prime said he saw the both of you leave from the Justice this evening. Where did he go afterwards? Did he say? Please!" He drooped.

She could hardly focus on what he was saying over the many voices of the godhead coming in. A breeze passed through the open window, bringing with it the smell of her old garden, when vegetation grew. Her fingers were harder to splay, making it nearly impossible for her to scratch the flesh giving way to sleek black beneath.

There was a splash in the basement, a woman's aching yell followed by a series of grunts. Maryja flashed an ironical smile; Idris looked unsteady. She had forgotten why they were all sitting there; it must have been important for her routine to be interrupted. She almost got up to boil some water but then didn't.

The fat red one slapped her face, and she screamed, from shock rather than pain.

"What of it? Do you want me to go looking for him? I can do nothing! He could be anywhere; he could be lost—"

Maryja had the urge to giggle, like a girl with a silly secret.

"You can't find him yourselves? I thought you could do anything!" The laughter slipped out, quickly stuffed back inside.

"Damn you, you serpent! If you don't answer, you'll be hung tonight!" He knocked the rest of the cups from the table, the whirlpools sucking her legs and toes together.

The sensation moved up to the narrow opening between her legs, making her moan.

"Viktor, patience is needed, patience—"

Idris heeled before her. "Is that what you have to say for yourself?! Why would he leave so suddenly? He had just arrived. Did you say something to him?"

"Maryja, please, where is my son?!" He puddled onto the floor.

Maryja couldn't hold her laughter any longer. It overtook her, writhing her out of her seat. The house rumbled, laughing with her. Even the basement grunts couldn't but join in. Idris howled, grabbing Maryja by the shoulders and throwing her against the wall. Her limbs coiled, making her laugh harder.

"What is that note? What did you do to my son?!"

The godhead had shown her what was funny, and why; it would cease to be humorous had she tried to explain it to them, who knew and saw nothing. She couldn't understand its ten-billion-year-old tongue, but the geometric cycles of time crashing into each other— resulting in innumerable happenstances— reminded her of the old slapstick movies that she and her mother used to enjoy, expressive black-and-white people fumbling and falling, one clumsy mistake leading to an utter debacle.

The young Fellow retrieved a vial from his pocket, his hand shaking. "Smell this, it will calm your—"

The oil slipped from his hand, coagulating the spilled coffee. It was the scent of lavender petals— earthen tender, too delicate and cloying to last. She smeared herself with the mixture, to soothe the prickling. Entranced by her wild tessellations, the men either didn't notice or react to her skin sloughing off in fractal patterns.

She saw each moment—dormant memories forever preserved— existing beside each other all at once. They had always been there, patient for her recognition like the pickled jars downstairs. She already knew which ones she wanted, picking them off the endless shelves of time, biting into the sour and swallowing what lay ahead.

"Don't you remember?" she whispered to Idris, "When we laid together, in his bed, when he was a baby— you put him on the floor, and he cried the whole time—" She mimicked his puling, still laughing.

The room across from hers rumbled, this time from pain.

"You never told me what happened to your first Servile, how she died. And your firstborn? The girl?"

"Never mind that!" Looking behind him, Idris too heard the nether entrance, his face bloodless. "Where's my boy, Maryja? I'll grant you your damned freedom— just tell me where he is!" He dropped into the bitter-sweet communion, sullying the Fellow's cassock.

"He's back inside me."

Maryja broke into hysterics, shivering as the last of her skin shed. Scales ran the length of her arms and ribs, fusing them. Only her neck and face remained of a woman. Idris swiped at her, to grab a chunk of her hair, coming from her scalp without resistance. He stood over her, an erection pressed against his pants, ready to behead her.

The mousy Fellow tried to scurry away. Cheeks engorged, Maryja lunged. His cassock caught the chair, black suit unfolding. Fangs penetrated his squeaking throat, curling his body covered in soft brown pelage head to foot like a fetus.

Opened and ready, she ate him.

The fat one squatted on the table. Haunches swollen, he flared his big red snout, canines at the ready. Maryja made for the basement; he swung in, slamming the door shut. The room opposite hers stirred louder. The blonde was finally exhumed, her mad birth pangs bringing on their battle.

"It's the Tree!"

Maryja rose to his eye level, dodging his clawed swipes. She wrapped herself tighter around him, yaks hollowed from the crushing. Idris doubled over as she gorged herself, another imprint alongside the others.

Idris thrust a wet knife in her direction, without much confidence. She maneuvered easily from his lumbering dodges. Her eyes were different in its reflection, pupils less rounded. The tan of her skin looked more like fermenting soil, extracting the rot carried in her for so long.

"I want my son! Maryja! I want—"

A massive little hand thrust through the kitchen floor; the other, through the foyer. A baby wailed. Tiny lavender heads poking through the buds were leveled by a fat foot, as was the porch and Idris's wicker chair on the opposite end. The reddening Eye warmed the child's dome crowning through the roof, raining shingles across the block. Tilted as the waiting room fissured, Maryja and Idris descended, the baby sat in the tumult of glass and limp vegetables.

Idris tried to stand, but his spine crooked, pushing his front limbs to the ground. Bowed over— hackles raised— he snarled at Maryja, awkwardly lunging towards her. The baby grabbed his Minister's jacket, pulling off the badges they'd given themselves and chucking them at him, screeching. He tried to speak, but the infant had suckled the language from him, leaving only barks. Idris sniffed, sitting before her enormous stomach, obedient.

As she flailed the floor fragmented further, debris falling into the grave below.

The distinction between the concrete Ministry and the clouded garden briefly dissipated in the baby's tears and spittle. The brush where snakes digested their meals rustled, littered with yellow pages and cauterized branches, the dead white willow felled across the grass. Patches of florae that had missed the brunt of the destruction were already flowering again.

She closed her eyes, the breeze of the wilder rippling over her, the last of flesh drifting off into the breeze in powdery tufts like dandelions.

The black mother was no longer confined here; she no longer needed to reside in small waters when a dank body had just been vacated for her. In her place, beneath the frozen surface, was the old occupant. Face, arms, legs, never quite clean, cur smell iced to her forever.

She followed his scent back, circling Idris as he shed short dark hairs from scratching. Growling, he ran off at the sight of her. Homing in on him racing upstairs, her forked tongue remained at his heels as the house caved in. Her full belly made her slower than usual, but he could not outpace her, ill-matched to her cold fluidity.

She bit his heel and he winced. Letting him go, she wound back. He jumped onto the bed, tail wagging, eager to catch the snake. Shredding the rest of his clothes, he reveled in his feral body as a wild dog's.

From the window, she could see the Weeping Tree burst into flames. Gnarled bark danced the fire around the Ministries, the crackling adding a hoarseness to the laughter and screams and cries. Outlines darkening scattered through the blaze, ashed to the degree of their sins. She hissed gleefully.

The Eye had kept her promise, rifts in the expanse warmed and widening.

Idris's bedroom had been stripped of most of its color and shape. There was only the dilated passage left. The shattered mirror cast back countless shades of the bovine portrait everywhere, taking up the space of the world. She was content as the men carried on like bratty children, happy to have her baby back.

The Minister had taken her place, his voice emanating from inside the walls.

"Bojana— did you think I had forgotten you? Tell me, dear— is Werner with you? I was glad to see Klara again— I missed her too, our little *blume*.

Your beastly revenant has come to avenge you— have you been watching all this time? From below, from above— the Savior, my mother, misses nothing..."

Triumphant from the chase, the snake sprung, letting Idris catch her in his jaws since she was predator. Holding her gently, he laid her down on the bed like when Maryja was a young virgin. Crescent tail to mouth, Idris sniffed cautiously. He licked her slimy skin as she bit down, burrowing deep into his fur. His yelps were suffocated as the vitriol swelled his face and oozed his useless bones.

Shrunk into her realm, he was made food for the recovering garden. She had taken more men this night than she had in her life. Her vision was but blue and green, with no teeth but fangs. Stomach stretched to capacity, she sank into the complacent comfort of the mattress. Human names and expressions no longer existing to her, she could recall one thing no longer in her immediate line of sight— red.

The baby arrived, crawling towards the passage. Searching for the source of her father's voice, she grabbed the queen like a plaything, tossing her with careless delight. Overtaken by the spiraling passage, the room, the house, and the militant world of the Ministry would soon be replenished and set in order again by its mother.

Yggdrasil, Home Again

Thrown from the babe's grip, Marija spiraled downwards. The calcination had spread into the amniotic void, the only point of light continually out of reach. Weightless and without direction, she could not see any bottom to the ribbed tunnel. Her body now long and thin, life incalculably small and large— near and distant— continued in their revolutions as eons passed. Without ground, she couldn't know if she was falling slowly, or not, how long she'd been falling; if she'd always been falling, and if she would ever stop.

Eventually there came the dull grey and chill; the pungent sweet of gasoline, steaming goulash, a trace of expensive perfume. Marija found herself in the field behind the *paneláks*, wondering why she wasn't in the flat with her mother.

The atmosphere choked on the smoke rising from piles of ashes around the buildings. Something like snow returned to the earth in soft drifts. Marija tried calling out, her voice hollowed by the void in her chest emanating a subterranean rumble. Cries of babies behind closed doors interjected sharply as dogs barked ferociously and neighbors argued in circles, alarmed like trapped animals.

The colorless dim granulated as a shadowed figure appeared at the entrance of the center building. In its hands was a singed straw doll, holes for eyes stuffed with yellow paper. The storm came to a halt; Marija called out for her mother again. The figure pointed at her, mocking, lurching back inside.

Skipping past the jolty lift Marija followed the dolled hand up the stairs. The shadow, around her size, kept laughing and pointing, making taunting, guttural noises unintelligible. A familiar shame crept in, making her want to crawl somewhere and hide, though she couldn't understand what was being said. A bottle with a flaming rag burned on the fourth-floor landing; the figure jumped over it, Marija nearly burning her feet evading it. It ducked into the first flat on the right, slamming the door.

A sourceless draft at the nape of her neck blew the cold down her back, more numbing with each step. Marija still felt a presence hovering. It almost took form in the achromatic light filtering in through smudgy panels above her head.

At the other end of the hallway, an opening ajar spilled out a brighter luster. Flashes of angry projections, snipped arguments swarmed as she quickened her pace, afraid of some hand reaching out from rooms of doors and walls, to snatch her away forever. Upon reaching their flat she locked the door, dropping her shoulders and unclenching her teeth in a heave of relief.

A white dress and smaller blue were draped across a chair. Water ran, muffled. Yellowed books lay open on the table around flowers waiting to be quenched. Marija looked over the pictures on the walls of the garden her mother had left behind when Marija was just a baby; she would often dream that the lines they recited took place there.

"*Maminka? Jsi tam?*"

High maternal melodies bubbled up from the hum. The chair was still warm, the kettle on the stove hot. The running sound led to the bathroom, locked. Tears muffled by hands thundered into thick, violent sobs, passing in a short while.

"Marija, listen to me— it's not safe here. Follow me there. Don't be scared. I'll be waiting."

A heavy collapse rattled through ceiling, followed by cracks and screams and two more heavy droppings, though not as heavy as the first. Curt commands cut over the chaos of pleading, tearing, and shatters. Booted thudding above made Marija clench again, her head and eyes pounding with each step. Over and over, she threw herself towards Jana as it drew louder.

Furiously, she begged to be let in, desperately needing to believe. If she could just see her mother's face, red-haloed, she could more easily take in her words.

"*Dcera*, don't be afraid. You're not alone. You've never been alone. I'm always there."

A roared, buzzing numb washed over. Outside, a white van pulled up behind a large ash pile, hidden from view from the black armored trucks, flashing its headlights as Marija looked in its direction. The tenants on her floor were in pandemonium alongside the dogs. They flooded the stairwell, shoving and stepping over each other to meet the inevitable.

The dark trespassers cut through, firing at everything that made sound. The rush fell in succession, one after the other as the beating of drums. Littered with dusted smoke and paint chips, the carpet was plush between her toes. Her soundless breath projected in her ringing ears.

The headlights flashed more urgently. The boots were storming the hall now, to check the flats. Marija wasn't scared anymore. She could feel her mother steady herself, the tension protruding between the drips of the sink. Marija nodded. She hit the floor as the door splintered, bullets whizzing like shooting stars.

Taking cover in the green lush, the bristles rose taller; she sunk through them as the grey world gave way to night.

The moon loomed over verdure and rolling hills in slumber, an invisible density pressed over the landscape. Punctured, the foremost hill bled with a gaping ochre wound in a cavern entrance. Marija tread out from it with bare feet onto soft, sharp grass, descending into a long stretch of field before the forest ahead. A metal fence separated them starkly.

She felt she was supposed to be meeting someone soon. Instead of a face or name, lines of vague poetry stuck:

'A snake without snake; a love without love—'

Marija was damp and uncomfortable and her side ached. She instinctually made for the wood, its trees with her secrets intricately woven in their canopies, that would reveal to her what she was supposed to be doing there. But the further on she went, the farther back it was pushed, the bark tapestry reduced to artful strokes. The silver-white pour widening blurred the distinction between day and night— above or below, the top or bottom of the scene.

She then noticed the holes— colors without dimension— in her arms and legs and face, painted incomplete. One in the field caught her ankle, trapped in her directionless outrunning to nowhere.

Each breath and movement were not her own, but fashioned by another. As the holes in her were filled, she stiffened. The call of a young woman's voice behind her rung out, but she couldn't turn to look. She penetrated the wood with a final gaze, at the black outline of a doe, emerging from its shelter to feed.

Distance compressed outside the portraits' field of view, framed off and nailed to some surface.

The subterranean vibration was much louder now, as the rush of a gorge or river. A deep sadness for that which was never to be reached tunneled the void from her chest inward, separating Marija from her vessel into wet fermentation. Florae, trees, and many worlds flourished in a ring encircling her. Cycles bloomed and died and bloomed again, so rapidly it felt like drawing breath. Their veiny roots twisted into each other, connected to one of three pulsing arteries boring under the widest expanse of all, holding up the plane.

Marija rose from the ground before a domed tree. The life amongst the flowers there were shaded by its tangled branches. A girl's screaming laughter was continually chased by the loud teasing of boys. Blonde marigolds growing in loamy soil buzzed with insects as blue irises, unable to drink the sun, wilted in the shade. Above the creatures resting and grazing a vulture circled overhead, anticipating the scent of blood.

Upon each branch the same play began many times simultaneously, each with a different ending— some victorious, some banal, some terrible. A wail— source of the vibration— trembled the tree, raining leaves and sticks to the ground. Birds sang their mourning dirge as the other creatures retreated into the trunk. Above everything was the reddish orb, patiently surveying her offspring.

Marija stepped out of the dome. Poppies had popped up between the dried blades. Static hisses, almost voices jutted out, leading her through the plane. The only others on her path, a cow and her yearling, glassy-eyed chews watching her until she was out of sight. After much walking, so far that the tree and anything but flat miles disappeared, she collapsed.

A brownish snake approached, coiling at her head.

One little lavender bloom had managed to hide amongst the red. The petals felt soft between her fingers, like soft fingers when she touched it to her breast. Her loins released a little death; she spasmed briefly, readied for a rest that would not force her awake again. She dreamt of another tree— one that had veiled her from the rest of the world, joys and sorrows, endless reveries performed for an audience that existed nowhere but for them.

After the fall, fat pinkish flesh rounded the horizon.

Before the baby, a pile of flaming snakes reached into the firmament, wrestling to escape. It put the final one, long and glossy black, atop the peak. Hot licks wrapped themselves around the vulgar forms, the infantile clapping in delight.

At the zenith, she was close to her mother again, warm and round. Millions of tendrils illuminated formed the outline of a face on fire.

She would be safe there soon.

About the Author

Daniela Králová is an author, poet, and musician based in Connecticut. Her novella, Maryja, a finalist in Digging Press's 2023 Chapbook Contest and a semi-finalist in Coverfly's 2024 Killer Shorts Contest, is now available at all major book retailers. Her latest works are featured in Connecticut Bard's Poetry Review via Local Gems Press. She can be found on Instagram @dmkralova.

Read more at https://dkralova.wordpress.com/.